W9-CEN-048

Missing Math

A Number Mystery

written and illustrated by

LOREEN LEEDY

Marshall Cavendish Children

Marshall Cavendish Corporation, 99 White Plains Road, Tarrytown, NY 10591
www.marshallcavendish.us/kids

Library of Congress Cataloging-in-Publication Data

Leedy, Loreen.
Missing math / written and illustrated by Loreen Leedy. -- 1st ed.
p. cm.
Summary: Everyday activities come to a halt when a town loses its numbers.
ISBN 978-0-7614-5385-7
[1. Numbers, Natural--Fiction. 2. Stories in rhyme.] I. Title.
PZ8.3.L4995Mi 2008
[E]--dc22
2007011718

The text of this book is set in Fink.
The illustrations were digitally painted using Adobe Photoshop.
Book design by Loreen Leedy
Editor: Margery Cuyler

Printed in China
First edition
1 3 5 6 4 2
Marshall Cavendish Children

To all the math lovers who will notice that "no" is equivalent to "zero"

Last Monday was an average day.
It wasn't odd or weird—
till numbers all around our town
completely disappeared.

They zoomed away in one big SWOOSH

and left a total mess.

The problems we are having now

are simply numberless.

Numberless: too many to be counted

We try to write more numbers down
with pencil, chalk, and pen.

But even when we think them up,
they slip away again.

So none of us can count amounts,
add numbers, or subtract.

And nobody can multiply.
THAT is just a fact!

We HAVE to find our numbers.
They could be anyplace.

The best detective in our town
is working on the case.

Lots of nuts...
but no numbers.

Our teams don't bother playing sports
like football anymore.

What's the point of playing games
if you can't keep the score?

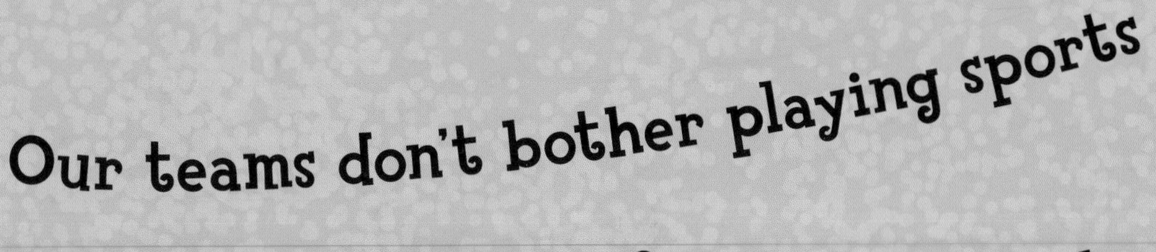

The TV channels left for good.
We tossed out our remotes.
And no one gets elected here
since we can't count the votes.

Our piggy banks are full of coins
to spend on something nice.
But money has no value now,
and nothing has a price.

We can't send mail or packages

by truck or boat or air.

Without the right address and stamp,

they can't go anywhere.

ME, MYSELF, AND I
? WHEREVER LANE
YONDER, WA ?

MISS JO NOBODEE
? SOMEWHERE STREET
ANYPLACE, FLORIDA ?

No street numbers,
no ZIP codes, and
no postage.

Should we wake up? Or go to bed?
When should we come or go?

Because our clocks can't tell the time,
we have no way to know.

Our calendars have empty squares,
so who can tell the date?

This might be April, May, or June—
we'll have to estimate.

Estimate: to make a rough guess

I hope my birthday's coming soon.
When will my party be?
She's still a calf.

I wish I Knew how old I was– what an EMERGENCY!

We checked these books out long ago.
It's hard to say quite when.
We'll keep them for a year or more,
then read them all again.

Our dinner tastes peculiar, but it isn't Daddy's fault.
His cookbook has no quantities—he put in too much salt!

The buttons on the phone are blank.

I can't call anyone!

The phone book is no help at all

This isn't any fun.

Computers stay asleep all day.
They will not operate.

The calculators are upset.
They cannot calculate.

How tall am I? What do I weigh?
And what's my temperature?
Without a way to measure things,
we just don't know for sure.

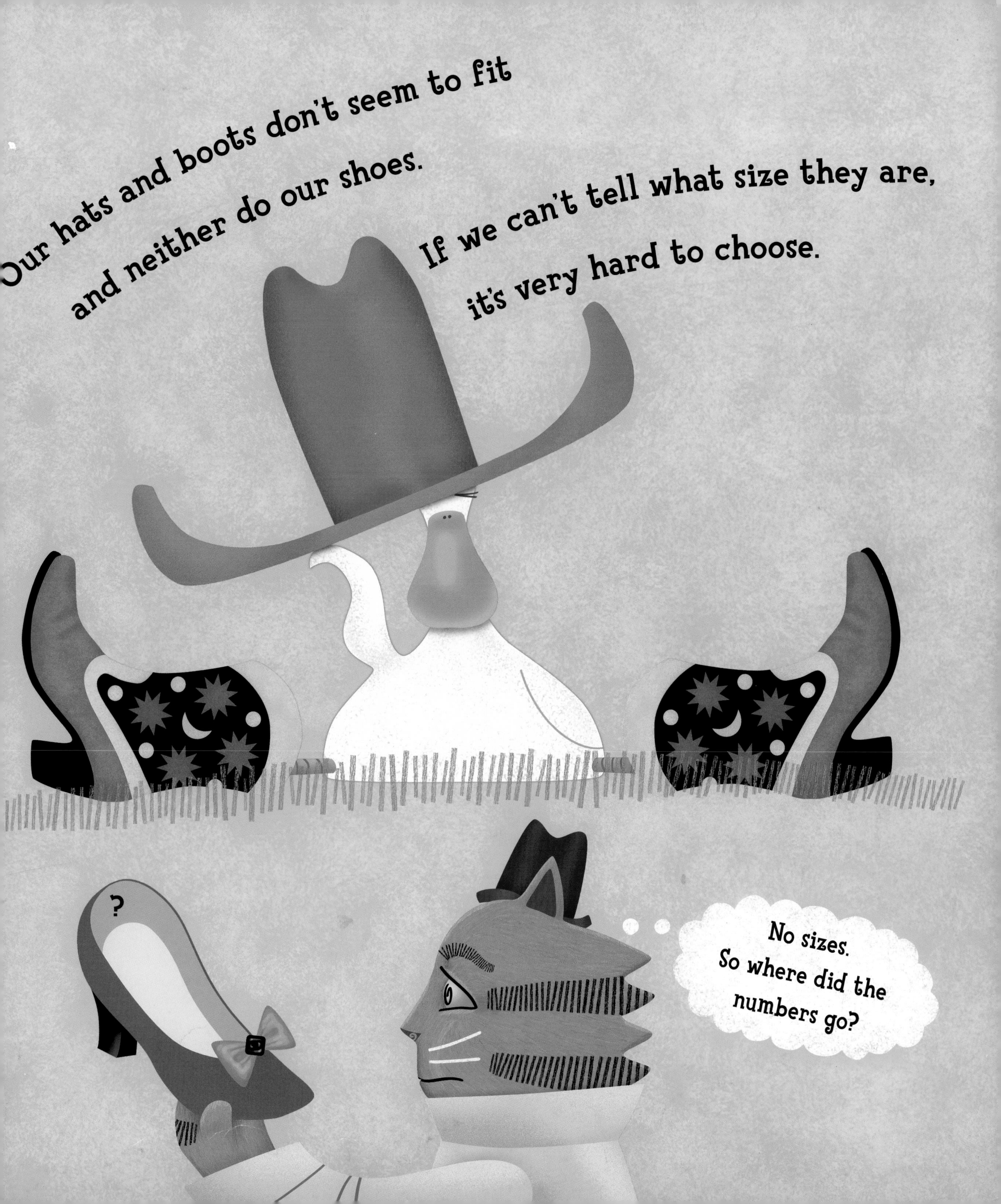
Our hats and boots don't seem to fit
and neither do our shoes.
If we can't tell what size they are,
it's very hard to choose.
?
No sizes.
So where did the
numbers go?

The workers who are building things
are in a frightful fix.
This brand-new house is nothing but
a crooked stack of sticks.

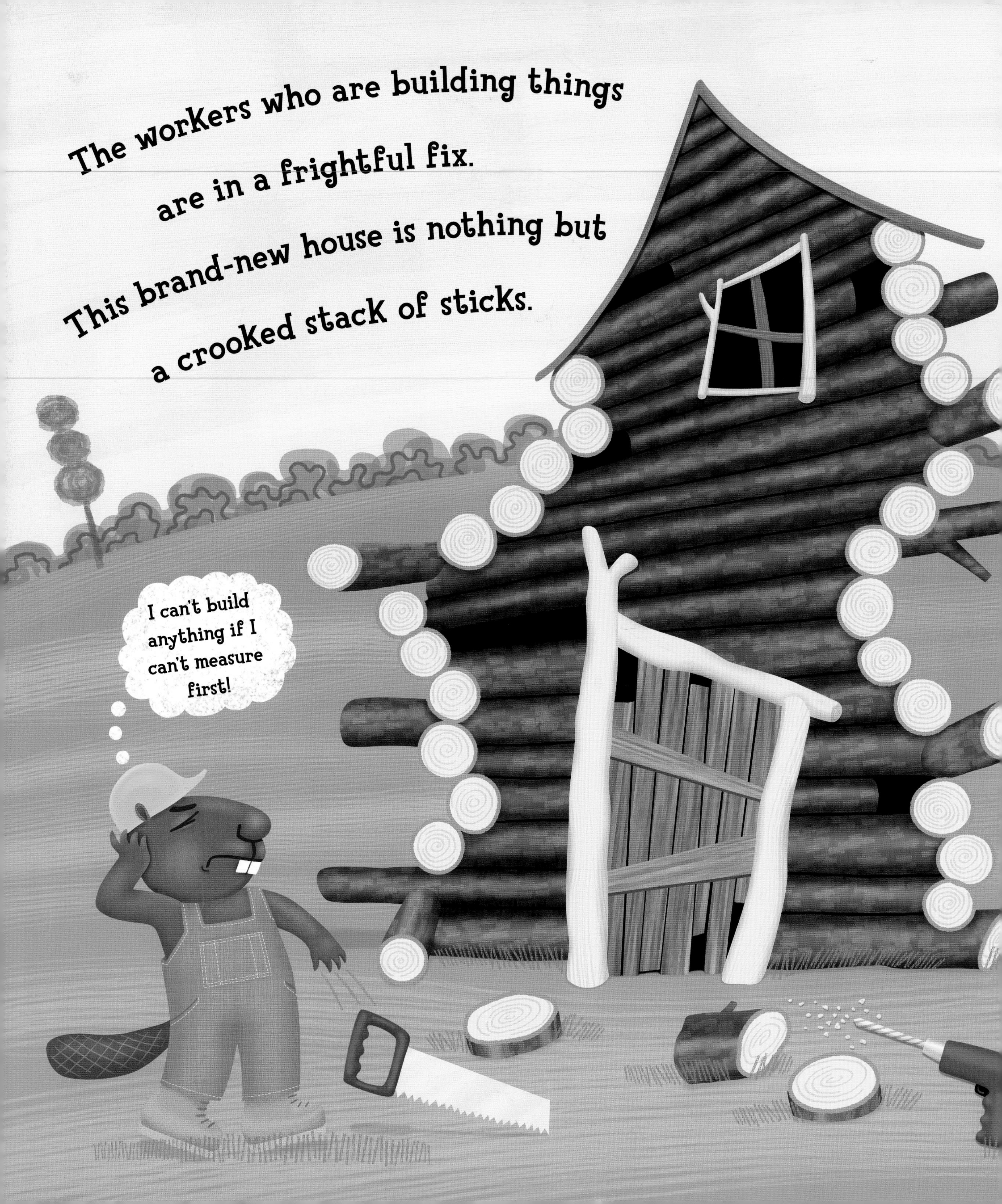

Can our detective solve this case?
It's very hard to wait.
Our numbers must be rescued soon,
before it's way too late!
SWISH!
What's that thing on the hill?
Let's go see–hurry up!

I've tracked you down, you number thief–
your number vacuum, too!
I want to ask a question, please.
What were you trying to do?!?
Let's put this vacuum into reverse.
IN
OUT
ON
OFF
THE NUMBER VACUUM
PATENT PENDING
4
7
3
8
5

To make the longest number that
the world will ever see,
I've been collecting numerals
to reach INFINITY.

Infinity: a number that never ends

Here's a ONE and there's a TWO,
a THREE and now a FOUR.
But math will be impossible
till we get several more.

A FIVE's arrived, a SIX and SEVEN.
EIGHT and NINE, hello!

And last, but not the least of all,
we welcome back ZERO!

It's time for us to celebrate!
We missed math every day.
Our numbers are at home again.
Math is here to stay– HOORAY!

1,001 DeLiCiOUS Doggie DiNNerS
Hello!

Isn't it great to have our numbers back?
Yes, but these library books are WAY overdue.
DON'T LEAF ME OUT: A TREE'S STORY
Speed Reading
PROCRASTINATION FOR BEGINNERS
The Life of a Slug
2+6=8
Your punishment is to fix all the phone books, so you'll need lots of glue.